TIGER!

PETER MILLETT · COLBY HEPPÉLL

Tiger!

Text: Peter Millett
Illustrations: Colby Heppéll Editor:
Rebecca Crisp
Design: Jennifer Warwick
Series design: James Lowe
Production controller: Lisa Porter
Reprint: Siew Han Ong

Fast Forward Independent Texts
Level 7

ISBN 978 0 17 017919 5
ISBN 978 0 17 017896 9 (set)

Cengage Learning Australia
Level 7, 80 Dorcas Street
South Melbourne, Victoria Australia 3205
Phone: 1300 790 853

Cengage Learning New Zealand
Unit 4B Rosedale Office Park
331 Rosedale Road, Albany, North Shore NZ 0632
Phone: 0508 635 766

For learning solutions, visit **cengage.com.au**

Printed in Australia by Ligare Pty Ltd
5 6 7 22 21 20

PETER MILLETT • COLBY HEPPÉLL

Contents

WHERE IS THE TIGER?

Josh and Ben were eating ice creams at the zoo.

"The bear looks hungry," said Ben. "He wants to eat my ice cream."

Josh laughed.

"No Ben, he wants to eat you!"

Ben laughed, too.

"Ben, where is the tiger?" asked Josh.

Ben looked down at the tiger's home.

"The tiger is not in its home," he said.

Josh cried out.
"Look – the door
to the tiger's home is open.
The tiger is out!"

CHAPTER 2

RUN!

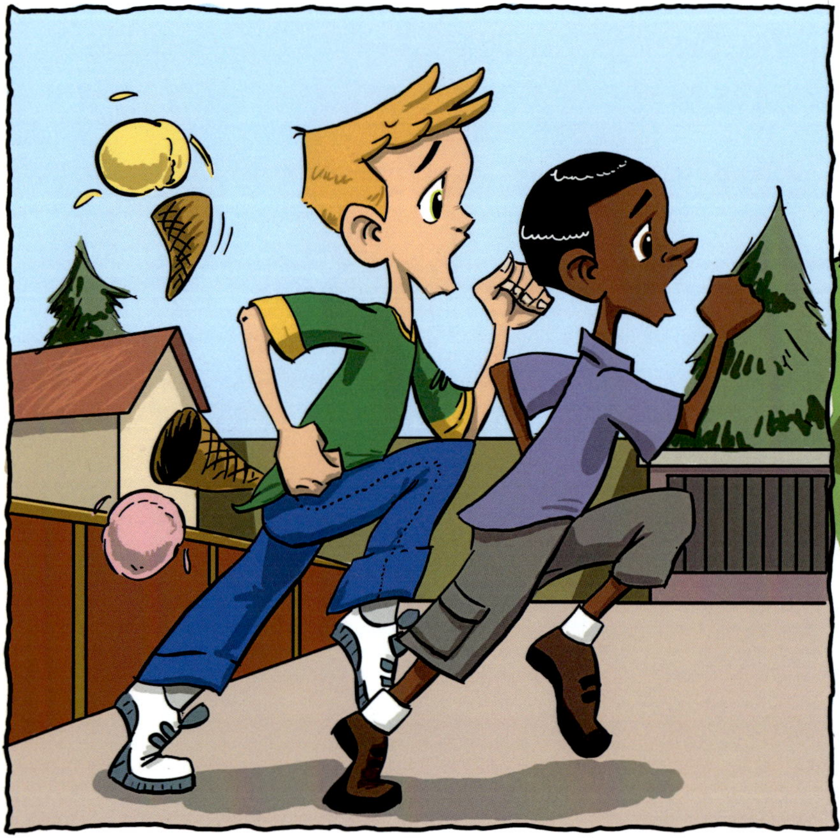

"Oh no, run!" cried Ben.

Josh and Ben ran away.

"Where is the tiger?" shouted Josh.

"Look! It's up in the tree," cried Ben.
"I can see the tiger's tail
in the leaves."

Josh and Ben looked up
in the tree.

Out came a monkey
that was hiding in the leaves.

"Oh, it's just a monkey," said Ben.

"Look!
It's hiding in the garden!"
cried Josh.
"I can see its eyes in the grass!"

Josh and Ben looked
at the garden.
Out came a house cat
that was hiding in the grass.

"Oh, it's just a cat," said Josh.

Then there was a loud roar.

"Run! It's the tiger!" shouted Ben.

Ben and Josh ran down the hill.

Josh looked around.
"No, no, it's a lion in its home!"
he cried.

ARE WE SAFE?

Then a truck came up.
The tiger was in the truck!

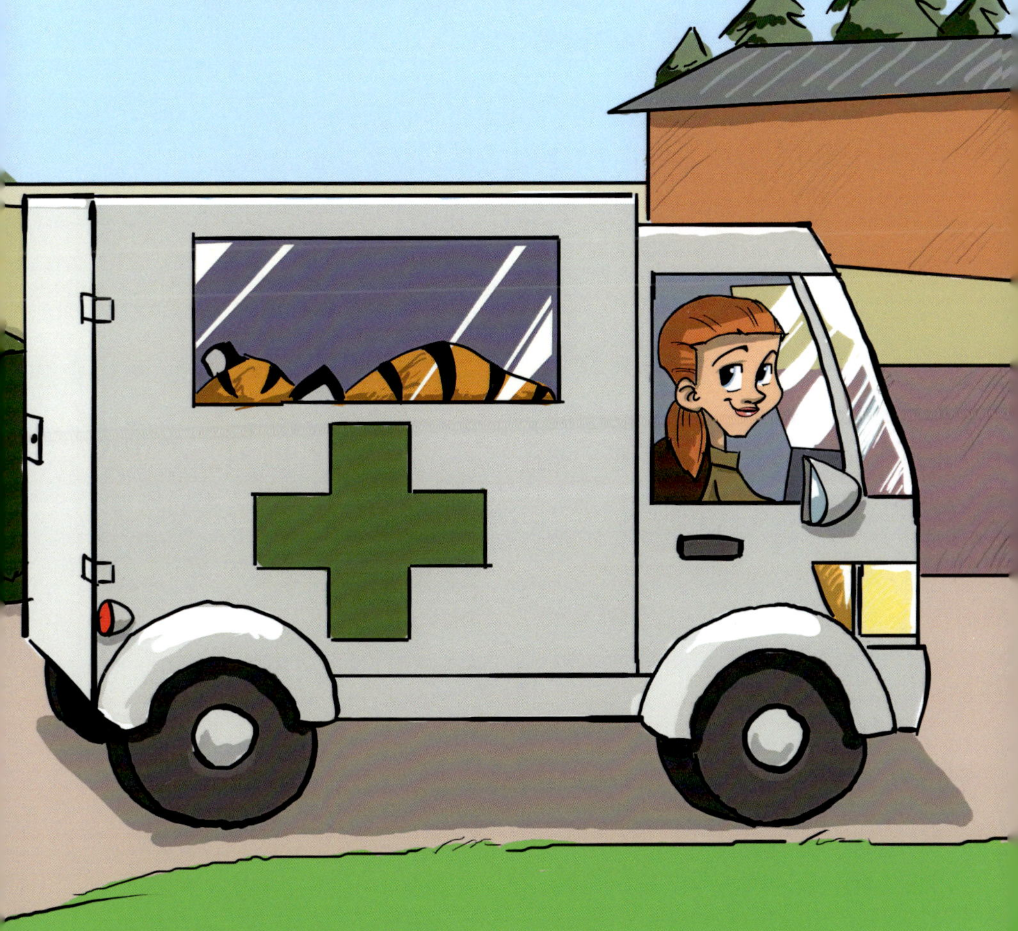

A woman opened the door.

"Oh no!" cried Josh and Ben.

The woman laughed
at Josh and Ben.
"You are safe," she said.
"The tiger is asleep,
but when he wakes up
– look out!
He will be *very* hungry!"